"Those Who Work The Land": The Three-Point Philosophy.

A Treatise drafted with Vigilance, Prosperity, Courage and Loyalty, laying out how the Empire is currently failing to recognise and reward those who **actually** keep the Empire Running

BY

Alfred Aewulfson

First Secretary of the Imperial Farmer's Union

Acknowledgements

To my Second & Third Secretaries Wulfrik
Wulfrikson & Doorhinge.
May the Virtuous Speed the Plough!

To my darling wife Ella
Thank you for putting up with me.

To the Anvil Book Club for your guidance and
support.

Contents

Preface

Before I start on this book, and the endeavour of laying out my thoughts on how the Empire unwisely continues to undervalue those who keep it running, I should start by saying that I am proudly and unabashedly a Farmer. I write this book from the perspective of a farmer who has been dispossessed by a sinkhole, lost half his crop to a horrific drought and was then subsequently flooded out of his farm by a Thunderous Deluge, and has recently had half his crop blighted by rogue Autumn magics.

For far too long, farmers have borne the brunt of the magical fallout of magic mischief, and due to having to continually fix damage to their livelihoods have remained on the periphery of recognition, their significance to the material of the Empire underappreciated and their contributions overshadowed by 'grander' professions. Yet, it is they who hold the real power to shape the destiny of the Empire, for food, flax and cloth is the lifeblood that fuels the Empire's progress. The Armies and Mages of the Empire may wield swords and conjure spells, but without sustenance, bowstrings or clothing to sustain them on campaign, their strength is nothing more than a flickering flame in the wind.

In a realm where the clash of swords and the grandeur of magic often dominate the tales of valour and adventure, this book instead seeks to shine a long-overdue light on the unsung heroes of our Empire - the farmers and those who work the land - whose unwavering dedication and tireless toil nurture the very foundation of our society.

This book is an attempt to right this historic wrong - It is a journey that delves deep into the heart of what the Author considers the real backbone of the Empire's prosperity, where the worth of a farmer's labour is unveiled. It is also a tribute to my brothers and sisters who till the soil and sow the seeds, who weave their skills and ply their craft in the fields to feed the hungry bellies of our people, and to the wider land-working population of the Empire – Miners, Herb Gardeners, Foresters, Mana Gatherers. You all work the land and you all deserve a greater share in the prosperity you generate.

I spend a large portion of my time as a farmer dealing with Marcher clients, as my farm as was used to border the Marcher territory of Mournwald, and they often spoke to me of Good Walder, a fine example of collective Prosperity, and whom the author believes should be spoken of more. Walder believed that hard work deserves reward, and that all those who take part in the work deserve a share of the rewards. It is a sad moment for me to have to write that I feel this example is not being heeded when it comes to securing prosperity for Farmers. For too long have farmers been instrumental to the success of Imperial campaigns, but hardly ever seem to see the rewards of their labour. It is time for us as a society to take stock and examine our own virtue, and work to correct where we may be falling short. To my mind:

- Is it not the **Courage** of a farmer to face the whims of nature and the market and place their trust in their ability as a skilled professional to make their crops rise successfully, especially with the added bane of rogue Mages?

- Is it not **Wisdom** that helps the farmer comprehend the intricate dance between the seasons and the crops? Is it not wise to also celebrate those who feed us and provide us with our clothing?
- What **Vigilance & Prosperity** do we claim to exercise if we cannot identify and punish those foolish Mages who cast rituals that ruin the lifeblood output of a farmer's toil, poured into every kernel of grain, with no thought beyond their own heroic assent?
- What **Loyalty** do we show by declaring 'this isn't my problem' or 'I don't care about farmers'? Both of these statements have been said to me on presenting the case of the Farmer's Union to those at an Anvil Summit.

In "Those Who Work The Land" I will lay out how we can reform the Empire to work better for those who seek to work the land, and through doing so aim to pay tribute to these unsung Heroes of the Mark and the Empire whose patience, perseverance, and unpretentiousness goes unrecognised. Theirs is a life entwined with an intricate understanding of the rhythms of nature, where hard labour and tireless effort allows them to provide for our homes and tables, and for this they receive meagre reward and little to no recognition.

In writing this work, I hope the Empire shall recognize the gravity of its oversight and the profound unvirtuousness in continuing not to recognise the thankless craft of farming. Let us mend the seams of this unjust tapestry, weaving instead a skien that bestows upon farmers the honour and appreciation they deserve. Together, we must rise above the shadows of ignorance, extending a hand of gratitude to the tillers of the land.

I hope that this work will serve as a rallying cry. May it pave the way for a new era, where the valour of farmers is heralded alongside the bravado of warriors and the brilliance of mages. Let us honour the farmers, the backbone of the Empire, and work together to give them and those who work the land a more prosperous future.

Part the First: From Ruin Spring Vigilance.

Imperial Service

My skein begins as a young Physick attached to the Blood Cloak army, and I spent a good chunk of my youth fighting for the Empire and bleeding for it in countless campaigns. I am proud when I tell you that I spent a good 8 years amidst the echoes of clashing swords, the resounding cries of battle and the long marches through hostile territory in pursuit of the Empire's goals. A proud soldier in the Imperial Army, my life had revolved around military drills, casualty clearance and treating the common ailments of the Imperial Army on campaign.

As the clangour of war resounded, I honed my craft as a battlefield surgeon, fighting through waves of Barbarians to reach the casualties who needed me most, and rendering the appropriate aid until they could be removed to an Imperial field hospital. Amidst the chaos and bloodshed, I embraced a different path for myself, a path where I chose to mend the wounded and alleviate suffering rather than seek a name for myself. Whilst I was not (and at time of writing am not) a sworn Grimnir, I believe there is wisdom in ensuring that good warriors live to fight again another day and tell their stories themselves. With steady hands and a compassionate heart, I tended to the injured, stitching wounds and staunching the flow of blood with a steadfast dedication to my craft as a Physick.

However, the price of fighting through to the wounded is oftentimes high to the physicks as well as the physicked. During the height of a battle, as my fellow healers were themselves locked in combat with a Jotun block, I found myself a casualty of their advances, struck from my blindside by a spear to my right knee. A sharp, wicked blade found its mark, slicing deep into my leg, leaving me wounded and vulnerable. Gritting my teeth against the pain, I pressed on to my casualty and withdrew them from the fray, refusing myself to become a casualty or succumb to the injury until I could see my patient to a triage area. Once done, I tended to my own wound and pulled myself out of the line, but at that moment I knew that my soldiering career was over and that my physicking would come too late to avoid permanent damage to my leg.

With this leg wound, which for the record has never fully healed, I chose with a heavy heart to bid farewell to the military life I had known and grown so fond of, and embarked on what I hoped would be a quiet retirement. All skeins must fork, and it seemed mine would soon see me out of the Imperial Army and in medical retirement. As I had done my time in the Imperial Army, and was retiring due to a wound sustained in battle, I claimed the parcel of land customary for retiring soldiers and put my skills in treating ailments and looking after patients into my new ambition - the role of a sheep farmer and local Physick to the village of Alnwick.

Catastrophe on Catastrophe

Retiring to the serene landscapes of the Hahnmark, I found comfort and purpose in tending to my flock which at its peak numbered more than 400 sheep. Each day, I would rise with the sun, tending to the needs of the sheep and cultivating the land that nurtured them. Yet, a skein of an Imperial Hero is never straight and untroubled. The year was 381YE, and Hahnmark was struck by an unfathomable catastrophe that shook its very core - the Hahnmark Sinkhole.

As the sun dipped beneath the horizon on that fateful evening, I had just finished shutting up the sheep for the evening and was beginning to make my way back to my house when the ground beneath my feet trembled with an unsettling intensity. Suddenly and with a crack like a Giant clearing it's throat, the earth gave way around me, swallowing the barn and a the whole flock of sheep. The Trigoni, the many limbed monstrosities that created the tunnels under the Sinkhole had awoken from their slumber, and over the next few days and weeks consumed vast stretches of fertile soil and fertile dreams with unyielding voracity.

Amidst the chaos and devastation, I found myself trapped in the midst of the catastrophe. The ground crumbled beneath me as I ran from the thundering earth, and in a flash, I was engulfed by the cascading earth. Struggling against the darkness, I fought for breath, my heart pounding in my chest as I battled to free myself from the suffocating embrace of the sinking earth. Drawing upon the resilience I honed on the battlefield, and telling myself

I didn't survive fighting against the Jotun for 6 years to be killed by a little mud, I summoned every ounce of my strength to claw my way towards the surface. With unwavering determination, I emerged from the suffocating depths, gasping for air and covered in the soil that had once nourished my livelihood.

My heart weighed heavy with the knowledge of the devastation that surrounded me. My farmland, my flock, and my future prosperity all lay buried beneath the sinkhole's grasp. It was a loss that cut deep, leaving me reeling from the impact of nature's indiscriminate fury. Whilst the initial shock reverberated far beyond the sinkhole itself, with many farmers across the region finding themselves facing the same tragedy, the Empire's response was lacklustre to say the least.

Senators refused to answer letters either because they were not reaching them or through indifference. Clients went elsewhere to secure wool contracts and prosperous use of the land was rendered impossible through repeated Tragoni attacks and the ravages of a campaigning Army of whom I had recently been a member. The naming rights to my farm were auctioned and sold without my knowledge. 'Lorenzo's Deep Pockets', it is called on Imperial maps. I found my funds dwindling, and my patience running thin.

From Ruin Spring Vigilance.

Across the barren landscape, I found common cause with fellow farmers who had endured the same fate. We found a stubborn tenacity to carry on, driven by the desire to see our prosperity restored and our treasuries renewed. It was during these difficult times that I again crossed paths with Wulfrik Wulfrikson, a former soldier-Physick of my old banner and another farmer who had also lost almost everything in the calamity. Drawn together by a shared tragedy, we formed an unbreakable bond of solidarity, and the seeds of the Wintermark Farmers Union sown in the heart of despair.

Wulfrik and I began talking and realised that we shared a common vision - the need for unity among farmers, a collective strength that would rise above adversity and build on the ashes of our former lives a greater prosperity of all who work the land, not just those who farm it. I was quickly appointed First Secretary of the Hahnmark Farmer's Union as it was on founding, with Wulfrik acting as my second and Doorhinge, a Varushkan purveyor of chemical concoctions and budding physick acting as our Treasurer.

We quickly set about rallying the farming community, appealing to their shared values of resilience and solidarity, a task that we find ourselves feverishly engaged in to this day. We have reached out to those whose spirits were shattered, offering them the opportunity to join a collective defence against rogue elements that will harm their bottom lines in the form of the Farmers Union. Together, our aim is to harness collective knowledge, pool experience and information, and advocate for our right to prosperity as hard-working farmers.

Through our hard work and determination, the Wintermark Farmers Union has grown exponentially, attracting like-minded souls who have rightfully recognised the worth and virtue of farming. Our calloused hands, once scarred by battle, now found new purpose in tilling the soil and sowing the seeds of vigilance against unwise action. We at time of writing number over one hundred proud farmers of Hahnmark, with a great percentile of those possessing the material means to also attend Anvil and have their voices heard.

Part the Second: Foundations and Thinking

Afflictions and Affectations

On reading this far, it would not surprise you to learn that the origins and genesis of my thoughts on the Way and how we can uplift the Farmers of the Empire comes from my own experiences of having the magicians of Conclave deliberately or through a complete lack of vigilance harm my livelihood repeatedly.

In the last 4 years, farmers have been afflicted or almost afflicted by:

- Horrific drought that made the land resistance to working, burnt crops or killed livestock.
- Thunderous deluges that flooded fields and washed-out crops/drowned livestock.
- boggarts and malign influences that vary wildly between helping with minor improvements to the land at extortionate cost at best, and straight up eating the children of the farmhands at their worst.
- Leaguish Wolves rampaging and eating livestock and children.
- a potential deal that Conclave had dreamt up that would have completely destroyed all agriculture to allow us to declare amity with Lofir, an Eternal.
- Rampant Autumn magic that has reduced some crops to literal dust.

- Any number of magical maledies that Conclave are dreaming up as I write.

These experiences of having the magicians of Conclave inadvertently or intentionally cause harm to my livelihood have left an indelible mark on me. It is clear to me as I reflect on the teachings of the Way that the role of pride within the magical circles of their own magical ability appears to be trumping other virtues like vigilance or loyalty. How can one be truly virtuous if they disregard the consequences of their actions on those who toil in the fields to sustain the Empire? Should we not hold ourselves accountable for the ramifications of our decisions, even when they seem distant from our immediate pursuits?

The Way teaches us that the pursuit of virtue must extend beyond just personal gains and encompass the betterment of the Empire as a whole. Magicians must embrace the merits of wisdom and apply some empathy before they look to cast a massive ritual, acknowledging the interconnectedness of their actions with the lives of all citizens. Only then can we truly uplift everyone who works the land, recognizing the sanctity of their craft and the importance of their role in shaping the destiny of the Empire.

It is only through mutual respect and collaboration that we can ensure prosperity **for all** within the Empire. Through my own experiences, I have come to realize that the Empire's true strength lies not just in its powerful magicians or valiant warriors, but in the unity of all its citizens. I envision a future where the Empire's magicians stand united with its farmers, working hand in hand to build a society that embraces all virtues, respects all crafts, and speeds all souls through the Labyrinth. Together, we can forge a legacy that embodies the true essence of the Way - a prosperous, vigilant and loyal Empire that thrives on the interconnected strength of its diverse talents, with farmers proudly and rightfully holding their place as the backbone of our prosperous nation.

The Three-Part Plan

I have over the last few years come to hold a trenchant opinion on the above, and have come up with a simple philosophy that I now intend to apply to all of my dealings with those who wield power and influence in the Empire. It is merely a summary of the above into three succinct points that, if followed, should all those who work the land to uplift themselves and challenge the dangerous uses of magic that blight our society.

My philosophy is simple, and can be summarised in three succinct points:

- **Point One:** Those who work the land **must receive appropriate reward for their work**, and must be able to seek assistance if they are dispossessed through the actions of Conclave/The Senate/insert body of state here.
- **Point Two:** Those who work the land **must have ready access to legal and financial aid** in times of strife to secure their prosperity, and exercise a means of collective vigilance against actions that would damage our livelihoods. They must have **recourse against those who damage their**

livelihoods, through misadventure as well as malice.

- **Point Three:** Those who work the land must have the right to **withdraw their labour** in protest and will refuse to support those who refuse to support them. Loyalty for Loyalty, Prosperity for Prosperity.

Those who work the land.

This work is meant not just to uplift farmers, but all who work the land in some way - encompassing all who work the land, regardless of their craft. The Empire owes its very existence to the dedication and toil of these unsung heroes. From the humble farmhand tilling the soil to the skilled artisan who bends the produce of the Miner into a beautiful sword, each individual plays a crucial role in nurturing the Empire's prosperity and is deserving of a reasonable share of that prosperity.

Those who work the land play an essential role in producing the goods and resources that sustain society. Their toil provides the necessary material basis for the functioning and advancement of the economy. The sweat of the laborers nourishes the seeds of the farmers, while the produce of the artisans sustains the Empire's populace. The intricate dance of these diverse talents creates a tapestry of abundance and resilience. The Way teaches us that Pride is not be reserved solely for those in grand positions or wielding great powers, but is extended to every individual who labours to make a difference. In this sense, those who work the land hold significant, and unrecognised, power and influence over the Imperial economy.

By fostering an environment of mutual support amongst those who work the land, we can break down the barriers that have historically divided us. Farmers, laborers, artisans, and all who work the land possess unique expertise and wisdom that can enrich the lives of others. Together, we can forge a path towards a more prosperous Empire. This work is not just a testament to the struggles faced by those who work the land, but also a celebration of their indomitable spirit. It is a call to action for us all to recognise the true worth of every individual's contribution and to embrace a collective responsibility for each other's well-being.

Pull together, not apart.

This is also not just about prosperity. Gaining appropriate reward and recognition should also be reflected in other aspects of the way the Empire and the various nations within in treat with those who work the land. We must overcome our differences as different professions and seek to build a universal approach where ALL those who work the land get this reward and recognition.

The Marches in particular could learn from this above point. I am not a Marcher, so I know little of their politics beyond what I have observed, but I have to say I agree wholeheartedly with Jed Boon of the Boon County Miners when he argues that as a miner, he should have the right to vote in a Marcher election. As Boon works the land, I see no difference between he who is disenfranchised and a farmer who can vote by virtue of working just the topsoil rather than the bedrock. This is an example where those who work the land should be pulling together to maximise their collective bargaining power rather than pulling in different directions through their vested interests. By working together, the Miners and Farmers of the Marches could ensure that both of these groups had their interests represented, and work together on matters of importance rather than pulling apart.

Part the Third: The Three Points Explored.

Point One: Appropriate Reward and Recognition

Appropriate Reward and Recognition is just that. Your labours as a farmer, a miner, a forester, a fisher should be rewarded for the service that they are – vital to keeping the Empire running. Appropriate recognition should hold significance and value. It goes beyond superficial praise and extends to expressions of appreciation that are sincere, personalised, and reflect an understanding of the individual's or group's efforts. This is sorely lacking in the Empire, with Farmers expected to just push through any difficulties they encounter with their harvests and with their livelihoods being damaged by harmful magic.

Empowering farmers and land workers will undoubtedly lead to better agricultural and industrial practices, increased yields, and greater resource security for the entire Empire. Thriving farms, mines and forests will lead to growth, stabilise food prices for those who cannot attend Anvil, and reduce our dependency on external supplies of these material sources. Because of this, I believe it is unwise to continue down a track where those who work the land face being routinely sacrificed on the altar of Eternals and experimental magic by Conclave - struggling farms, mines and forests means reduced output, which means more trade with our potentially treacherous and unstable barbarian neighbours, reducing our self-sufficiency as an Empire.

Resource security is not something I believe we currently seriously consider or plan for as an Empire, and to my mind that leaves us dangerously unprepared for and almost ushering in a situation where we cannot supply our armies due to the actions of the Empire itself. If we continue to harm those who work the land, they will simply stop working the land for other careers, and we will lose what little stretch the current supply has for our armed forces and their campaigning capacity.

If you work the land, you have the right to appropriate rewards for your labour, so **recognise your power in this regard.** You play a pivotal role in ensuring food security. You produce the crops and livestock that form the backbone of the nation's food supply. When farmers face challenges such as unpredictable weather conditions, pest infestations, or limited access to resources, food production can suffer, leading to potential shortages and higher food prices.

When those who work the land are adequately supported, they can increase their prosperity and with it their productivity, thus contributing to a more stable and secure food supply for the entire Empire. If they are not supported, they have the right to withdraw their labour and supply those who will be loyal to them.

Point Two: Through Misadventure as well as Malice

Access to legal and financial aid is **essential** for those who work the land to secure their prosperity and protect their livelihoods. In times of strife, whether caused by natural disasters or man-made challenges, having readily available support can be the difference between maintaining your prosperity and complete devastation.

By establishing mechanisms for legal and financial aid, farmers, laborers, and artisans must have the means to obtain assistance needed to recover from unforeseen setbacks. I already offer this aid in the form of low-interest loans to those who apply to my Union and I have already issued some loans to help my fellow farmers rebuild after disasters like the Thunderous Deluge.

Furthermore, a means of collective vigilance is crucial in safeguarding the interests of those who work the land. You should be looking to join an organized union or association for your particular profession. General unions like mine (The Imperial Farmer's Union) exist, but I know of several nation specific unions that are being formed to address these challenges. Join one! Through collective action and organization, those who work the land could challenge for a greater say in their respective nations and the Empire at large, and work together to advocate for greater prosperity.

Through them, those who work the land can unite to address shared challenges, negotiate for better rewards for their labour with suppliers and advocate for more safeguards against idiotic magic use. This collective vigilance empowers them to have a stronger voice in the face of adversity, ensuring their concerns are heard and taken seriously.

Recourse against actions that damages your livelihoods, whether accidental or malicious, is another critical aspect. By having channels to address disputes and seek compensation, those who work the land can protect their interests and hold accountable those responsible for any harm caused. This recourse ensures that they are not left defenceless against unfair treatment or negligence, fostering an environment of accountability and responsibility amongst those who cause the most harm. Wintermark has the tradition of Weregild, where compensation payments are made to the victim of a crime by the perpetrator.

I am proposing that the Empire adopts this system Empire-wide, allowing those citizens whose livelihoods are affected by rogue magic to pursue the Imperial Conclave for reimbursement of their lost prosperity. By making Conclave responsible for the damage caused by Magic, this should ensure Conclave takes a closer look at Empire wide casting of rituals. I also strongly believe that this should apply in cases where the damage was accidental as well as malicious – we need to establish greater safeguard against wanton use of magic.

In establishing these support systems and avenues for recourse, the Empire strengthens its agricultural sector and the well-being of its citizens. When those who work the land feel secure in their livelihoods and have access to assistance when needed, they can focus on their craft with greater dedication and it will boost their prosperity and their loyalty to their fellow citizens. This, in turn, contributes to the overall economic growth and stability of the Empire.

Point Three: Withdrawal of Labour.

When all other measures fail, those who work the land possess a powerful recourse in their hands—the ability to withdraw their labour and withhold the supplies that sustain the Armies and Fleets of the Empire. It is a profound step, signalling their importance and the critical role they play in the functioning of the Empire which often goes overlooked.

Such an action would not be taken lightly, for it comes with considerable consequences for both sides. The refusal to supply the Armies and Fleets could disrupt the Empire's military operations, affecting its ability to defend its borders and maintain order within its territories. It could also leave those taking part in this action open to accusations of subversion.

However, this ultimate recourse is a testament to the significance of those who work the land and the invaluable contributions they make to the Empire's strength and prosperity. It underscores their unity and determination to protect their livelihoods and seek appropriate recourse for any harm inflicted upon their livelihoods.

By holding firm and refusing to supply the forces of the Empire, those who work the land could hypothetically exert considerable pressure on the political establishment to engage in negotiations and address their grievances.

Such actions can lead to a dialogue with the goal of finding a fair and sustainable solution.

Moreover, the act of withdrawing their labour and supplies can serve as a wake-up call for the Empire's leadership, shedding light on the significance of the farming communities and the need to prioritize their well-being. It is a demonstration of their unity and collective strength, compelling the authorities to recognize and appreciate their vital role in the Empire prosperity.

In Conclusion

The ideas contained herein represent the first attempt by me to lay out my thoughts on how the Empire could better serve those who are crucial to the Imperial economy. By cultivating the land, they not only provide sustenance for our home population but also the logistical backbone of our armies in the field. As we close the final chapter of "Those Who Work The Land" we are reminded that the prosperity of the Empire lies not just in the grand gestures of its leaders or the accomplishments of its renowned figures. It is the collective efforts and unwavering loyalty of every individual, especially those who work the land, that sustain and uplift the Empire.

In this treatise, I sought to celebrate the unyielding spirit of those who work the land, and those who have weathered trials and tribulations with unwavering dedication. Their commitment to their craft and to the Empire is a testament to their Loyalty to an Empire that often overlooks their sacrifices and commitment. I believe my Three-Part Plan to be virtuous in intent, but I absolutely welcome challenge from those who wish to provide a counterpoint to my proposals for providing those who work the land with a better chance to build and sustain their prosperity.

As we move forward, it is crucial we as an Empire continue examining the conditions and well-being of those who toil on the land. Recognizing their contributions and addressing the inequities they face is vital for building a more sustainable future, where the significance of those who work the land, and just how vital they are to a functional economy, is upheld and celebrated.

Printed in Great Britain
by Amazon